Dear Parents and Educators,

Welcome to Penguin Young Readers! As parents and educators, you know that each child develops at his or her own pace—in terms of speech, critical thinking, and, of course, reading. Penguin Young Readers recognizes this fact. As a result, each Penguin Young Readers book is assigned a traditional easy-to-read level (1–4) as well as a Guided Reading Level (A–P). Both of these systems will help you choose the right book for your child. Please refer to the back of each book for specific leveling information. Penguin Young Readers features esteemed authors and illustrators, stories about favorite characters, fascinating nonfiction, and more!

Young Cam Jansen and the Ice Skate Mystery

LEVEL **3**

GUIDED READING LEVEL **J**

This book is perfect for a **Transitional Reader** who:
- can read multisyllable and compound words;
- can read words with prefixes and suffixes;
- is able to identify story elements (beginning, middle, end, plot, setting, characters, problem, solution); and
- can understand different points of view.

Here are some **activities** you can do during and after reading this book:
- Reading with Expression: Although many transitional readers can read text accurately, they may read slowly or not smoothly and pay little or no attention to punctuation. Read page 13 in this story out loud. Ask the child to pay attention to how your voice changes when you read the word *crash* and when you come across different punctuation such as question marks, quotation marks, and periods. Then have the child read another page out loud to you.
- Summarize: Work with the child to write a short summary of what happened in the story. What happened in the beginning? What happened in the middle? What happened in the end?

Remember, sharing the love of reading with a child is the best gift you can give!

—Bonnie Bader, EdM
  Penguin Young Readers program

D0311149

*Penguin Young Readers are leveled by independent reviewers applying the standards developed by Irene Fountas and Gay Su Pinnell in *Matching Books to Readers: Using Leveled Books in Guided Reading*, Heinemann, 1999.

To Renée, with love, happy Silver!

Penguin Young Readers
Published by the Penguin Group
Penguin Group (USA) Inc., 375 Hudson Street, New York, New York 10014, USA
Penguin Group (Canada), 90 Eglinton Avenue East, Suite 700, Toronto, Ontario M4P 2Y3, Canada
(a division of Pearson Penguin Canada Inc.)
Penguin Books Ltd., 80 Strand, London WC2R 0RL, England
Penguin Group Ireland, 25 St. Stephen's Green, Dublin 2, Ireland (a division of Penguin Books Ltd.)
Penguin Group (Australia), 250 Camberwell Road, Camberwell, Victoria 3124, Australia
(a division of Pearson Australia Group Pty. Ltd.)
Penguin Books India Pvt. Ltd., 11 Community Centre, Panchsheel Park, New Delhi—110 017, India
Penguin Group (NZ), 67 Apollo Drive, Rosedale, Auckland 0632, New Zealand
(a division of Pearson New Zealand Ltd.)
Penguin Books (South Africa) (Pty.) Ltd., 24 Sturdee Avenue, Rosebank,
Johannesburg 2196, South Africa

Penguin Books Ltd., Registered Offices: 80 Strand, London WC2R 0RL, England

The Library of Congress has cataloged the Viking edition under
the following Control Number: 97040256

ISBN 978-0-14-130012-2   10 9 8 7 6 5 4 3 2 1

LEVEL **3**
PENGUIN YOUNG READERS
TRANSITIONAL READER

Young Cam Jansen
and the Ice Skate Mystery

by David A. Adler
illustrated by Susanna Natti

Penguin Young Readers
An Imprint of Penguin Group (USA) Inc.

Contents

Chapter 1
Let's Skate

"I can't get my foot in,"

Eric Shelton said.

"Just push,"

his friend Cam Jansen told him.

"Ice skates should be snug."

Eric held onto the sides of the skate.

He pushed hard.

"It's in," he said.

He put on the other skate.

Then he tied them both.

Eric stood up.

"I feel so tall," he told Cam.

Cam stood.

She was wearing skates, too.

She was as tall as Eric.

Mr. Shelton, Eric's father,

was also wearing ice skates.

Cam, Eric, and Mr. Shelton

took their shoes off the bench.

"We have to put these in lockers,"

Cam said.

"I saw a sign when we came in."

Cam closed her eyes and said, "Click."

"Do not leave items on benches.

Rent a locker.

Lockers 25 cents."

Mr. Shelton looked at the sign.

Mr. Shelton told Cam,

"That's just what it says."

Eric told his father,

DO NOT LEAVE
ITEMS ON
BENCHES

RENT A LOCKER
LOCKERS
25 CENTS

"Cam has an amazing memory."

Cam opened her eyes.

"My mind is like a camera," Cam said.

"I have a picture in my head
of everything I have seen."

Cam says "click" is the sound her
camera makes.

Cam's real name is Jennifer.

But because of her amazing memory,
people started calling her
"the Camera."

Then "the Camera"
became just "Cam."

Mr. Shelton gave Eric a quarter.

Cam and Eric put the shoes

in a big locker.

Eric put in the quarter.

He closed the locker door.

He turned the key and took it out.

Mr. Shelton said, "Let me hold the key."

Eric was next to Cam.

"I'm not a baby," Eric said.

"I won't lose it."

He put the key in a jacket pocket.

"Let's skate," he said.

Chapter 2
Crash!

Cam, Eric, and Mr. Shelton went

onto the ice.

They held hands and

skated together.

"Faster!" Eric said.

Cam and Mr. Shelton skated faster.

"Faster! Faster!" Eric said.

"I can't go any faster," his father said.

Eric skated ahead.

He skated around a group
of children.

He went between a boy and girl.

There was a large group
of skaters ahead.

They were all holding hands.

Eric skated quickly around them.

He skated into the rail.

Crash!

Eric fell onto the ice.

Cam, Mr. Shelton, and a man in a green jacket rushed to Eric.

"Are you hurt?" Mr. Shelton asked.

Eric looked up at his father.

Eric slowly shook his head.

"You were going too fast,"

Mr. Shelton told him.

"No," Eric said.

"It was the rail.

It was going too slow."

"That's not funny," Mr. Shelton said.

"You must be more careful," said
the man in the green jacket.

He worked at the rink.

Mr. Shelton helped Eric up.

"I'll skate with you," Cam told Eric.

"Go slowly."

Cam and Eric skated together.

They went around the rink

a few times.

Then the voice from the loudspeaker

said, "This session will end

in three minutes.

Please return to the locker room."

Cam and Eric skated to the exit.

They were ready to get off the ice.

Eric reached into his pocket.

"Oh no!" Eric said.

"The key is gone!"

Chapter 3
Let's Go! Let's Go!

"Check your pocket," Cam said.

"Maybe there is a hole in it."

Eric reached into his pocket.

He turned it inside out.

"There is no hole," he said,

"and no key."

Cam said, "Maybe you lost it

when you crashed into the rail."

"Maybe," Eric said.

He looked around the rink.

"But I don't know where I fell," he said.

Cam closed her eyes and said, "Click."

She looked at the picture in her head.

"I know where you fell," Cam said.

"Where the letters M L are painted on the rail."

Cam opened her eyes.

She and Eric skated slowly

around the rink.

They found M L painted on the rail.

They did not find the key.

"Let's go! Let's go!"

the man in the green jacket said.

"I lost my key," Eric told him.

"You may take a quick look
before you go inside,"
the man said.

"I'll make an announcement."

Chapter 4
Click! Click!

Cam and Eric skated

around the rink.

They found a red mitten

and a blue scarf.

They did not find the key.

They went into the locker room.

Soon they heard the announcement:

"A red mitten, a blue scarf, and a

key have been lost.

"Please return anything you found
to the office."

Cam and Eric returned the mitten
and scarf.

They waited at the office.

A boy came for the mitten.

A woman came for the scarf.

But no one returned the key.

Mr. Shelton saw Cam and Eric.

"There you are," he said.

"Let's get our shoes from the locker.

We can get pizza on the way home."

Eric looked at Cam.

Then he said,

"Not yet, Dad.

Please, can I get a cup of hot

chocolate?"

"Later," Mr. Shelton said,

"after we get our shoes."

"Please, Dad, may I have it now?"

Mr. Shelton smiled and said, "Yes."

Then he asked Cam,

"Do you want some

hot chocolate, too?"

"No, thank you," Cam said.

Eric and his father

went to the snack bar.

Cam sat on the bench.

She closed her eyes and said, "Click."

She looked at a picture in her head.

She was trying to find the lost key.

Cam said "Click" again.

Click.

Click.

Click.

Chapter 5
Come On, Dad

Cam looked at the pictures
she had in her head.
She saw Eric take the key
from the locker.
She saw Eric say he was not a baby.
She saw him put the key in his
jacket pocket.
Cam said "Click" again.
Then she opened her eyes.

She put her hands in her pockets.

"Eric! Eric!" she called.

Eric hurried to Cam.

"Sit next to me," Cam said.

Eric sat on the bench next to Cam.

"No," Cam told him.

"Sit on my other side."

Eric moved to Cam's other side.

Cam said, "Now reach into
your pocket."

Eric reached in.

"It's empty," he said.

"Reach in again," Cam said.

Eric reached into his pocket again.

"It's still empty," he said.

"Reach in again," Cam said.

Eric reached in and said, "Oh!"

He took out a key.

"How did this get into my pocket?"

"It wasn't in your pocket,"

Cam said.

"It was in mine.

We were next to each other before, too.

You thought you put the

key in your pocket.

You really put it in mine."

Eric used the key to open the locker.

He took out the shoes and called,

"Come on, Dad.

Let's put on our shoes."

He gave his father the key.

"You were right," Mr. Shelton said.

"You are not a baby."

"Of course I'm not a baby," Eric said.

"I can skate.

I can ride a bicycle.

And I can read."

Eric smiled.

"And I can eat pizza.

Let's go!"

A Cam Jansen Memory Game

Take another look at the picture on page 4.
Study it.
Blink your eyes and say, "Click!"
Then turn back to this page
and answer these questions:

1. Is Eric smiling?

2. What color is Eric's jacket?

3. What color are Cam's skates?

4. What color are Cam's pants?

5. Is there anyone in the locker
room?